The Bridegroom Was a Dog

Yoko Tawada

Translated by Margaret Mitsutani

GRANTA

Granta Publications, 12 Addison Avenue, London W11 4QR

First published in Great Britain by Granta Books in 2024
This paperback edition published by Granta Books in 2025

First published in the United States in 2012 by
New Directions Books, New York

This translation of *The Bridegroom Was a Dog* (*Inumukoiri*)
was originally published in 1998 by Kodansha Ltd., Tokyo

A CIP catalogue record for this book
is available from the British Library.

1   3   5   7   9   10   8   6   4   2

ISBN 978 1 80351 133 7
eISBN 978 1 80351 134 4

Typeset in Arno Pro by Patty Rennie
Printed and bound by CPI Group (UK) Ltd, Croydon, CR0 4YY

www.granta.com

The manufacturer's authorised representative in the EU for product
safety is Authorised Rep Compliance Ltd, 71 Lower Baggot
Street, Dublin D02 P593, Ireland. www.arccompliance.com

The Bridegroom
Was a Dog

The mid-afternoon sunlight stuck, pure white, to the vertical and horizontal washing on the lines as an old man, walking through a large apartment complex in the airless, clammy heat, suddenly stopped in the middle of the road to look back over his shoulder and froze that way, and a brick-red car ground to a halt beside a mailbox as if its strength had petered out, though no one got out into the stillness of a July day at two o'clock, silent except for a distant drone that might have been either a dying cicada or the hum of a machine in a school-lunch factory.

In a six-mat room beyond the railing on her balcony a housewife was making tea, stopping now and then to frown at the blank TV screen as she picked at a scab on her knee; her neighbor, who had gone to the local Culture Center, had closed her kitchen curtains but not all the way, so you could see a half-eaten apple with lipstick stains on top of the refrigerator. In one corner of this apartment complex in a modern residential area, so dull it seemed dead until the children came home to get ready for cram school, there was a large, dirty homemade sign that had been clinging to a telephone pole for a year or more, always seeming about to fall off but somehow stubbornly managing to stay on. The rain had blurred the words "Kitamura School," written with a pink magic marker in Mitsuko Kitamura's handwriting, and the telephone number was half torn off, and there was so much yellow pigeon shit stuck to the map you could hardly read it, but since all the mothers in the complex with children of elementary or junior high school age knew where the Kitamura School was this didn't pose a problem, and although the poster had outlived its usefulness no one bothered to dispose of it, either because it was too filthy to touch, or out of loyalty to the tradition, firmly established in the thirty years since the complex had been built, of not worrying about how dirty things outside were as long as the area around your own apartment was clean, which meant that when a pigeon was hit by a car and lay splattered all over the street or some drunk left a pile of turds somewhere, people just waited for City Hall to clean it up, so naturally no one could have cared less about this sign, which would prob-ably stay there until the wind ripped it to shreds and blew it away.

Anyway, the children all loved the Kitamura School, which they nicknamed the "Kitabooboo School"; in fact, so many wanted to go there it had become something of a fad, and even if it failed to improve some kids' grades, with all the stories these days about youngsters enrolled in cram schools they hated but actually spending the time in Game Centers, it was a relief to mothers, knowing they didn't have that to worry about with the Kitamura School, so most didn't let the strange rumors bother them, and when someone occasionally was heard saying she'd *never* send one of her children to a place like that, the others would tell her not to get so excited about some idle gossip which was only a kid's imagination to start with, blown out of all proportion, and since children can't really tell the difference between a little dirt and downright obscenity and tend to get things mixed up anyway, it was best not to believe everything they said, etc., etc.

Take, for example, what some grade school kids were reporting to their mothers about "snot paper": "Miss Kitamura says wiping your nose with snot paper you've already used once is nice, because it's so soft and warm and wet, but when you use it a third time to wipe yourself when you go to the bathroom, it feels even better." Mothers blushed to hear this from a son or daughter of theirs, wanting to scold but not sure exactly why or how, and in the end just telling them, "You mustn't say 'snot paper,' it's 'tissue,'" only to find that, no matter how determined they were not to imagine their child's beautiful teacher sitting on the toilet wiping herself with that lovely moist tissue, Miss Kitamura's smiling face invariably rose before them. And this, in turn, would remind them what the head teacher at the elementary school had said about her: "It's unusual for a beautiful woman to look that happy. I thought traditional beauties were supposed to be sad and lonely." Regardless of whether rumors about the head teacher's being distantly related to Mitsuko Kitamura were true or not, the mothers talked themselves into believing that if that straitlaced old schoolmarm said Mitsuko was beautiful, she couldn't be all that "dirty" and some even thought Mitsuko might be telling her pupils about "dirty" things on purpose, for educational reasons. And besides, none of the kids who had heard Mitsuko talk about the virtues of using "snot paper" three times followed suit and picked up an unhygienic habit; on the contrary, they were as wasteful as ever, rolling out reams of toilet paper so they could use just a few sheets at the end, and compared to the stories you heard about kids who competed with their little brothers to see who could pull the most tissues out of the box in the shortest time and then sent the whole wad fluttering down from the fifth floor window, Mitsuko Kitamura's lecture on "snot paper" began to sound like a serious lesson in frugality. So in the end no one took their children out of the Kitamura School because of the talk about "snot paper"; in fact, long after the kids had forgotten all about it, many mothers found that it came back to them every time they went to the toilet, and some wondered if there wasn't a softer, moister kind of paper they could use instead of this machine-made stuff, which felt awfully dry and scratchy sometimes.

What really stimulated their sensitivity in this area was the story the kids brought home about a princess and her dog. "Maybe the only story you know about a human being marrying an animal is 'The Crane Wife,' but there's another one called 'The Bridegroom Was a Dog'" Miss Kitamura began, and the children listened carefully until the end, but the tale was so long that the younger ones got mixed up when they tried to tell it at home, and the older ones were too embarrassed to repeat it, so curious mothers were left to piece together the fragments they'd overheard for themselves, but, anyway, the story went like this. Once upon a time there was a little princess who was still too young to wipe herself after she went to the lavatory, and the woman assigned to look after her was too lazy to do it for her, so she used to call the princess's favorite black dog and say, "If you lick her bottom clean, one day she'll be your bride," and in time the princess herself began looking forward to that day....

Up to this point in the story, the children's accounts all matched each other, but there were various versions of what happened next: some said, for instance, that one day the black dog kidnapped the princess and took her deep into the forest, where he finally married her, while others said the princess's parents flew into a rage when they happened to catch the black dog licking their daughter's bottom, and sent both of them into exile on a desert island. The forest version had a hunter who killed the black dog when the princess wasn't looking and married her himself, after which the princess, though puzzled at first as to why the dog should suddenly have vanished and this hunter appeared in his place, lived happily with her new husband until one night he mumbled something in his sleep about having killed the animal, where-upon she promptly picked up his gun and shot him dead. The desert island version also had a further episode in the princess's life: she gave birth to a son, after which the black dog got sick and died, so to keep the family line from dying out the princess had relations with her son and bore more children. This arrangement she cleverly brought about by telling the boy one morning: "Go around the island to the other side and take the first woman you meet there as your wife," and while he was following the coastline in one direction, she herself set out in the other, and when the son met his mother on the far side of the island he slept with her without know-ing who she was.

To the children listening, who didn't even know the word "incest," all this seemed perfectly natural, and it wasn't long before they'd forgotten all about it, whereas the part about the black dog obeying the lazy woman and licking the princess's bottom clean left a far more vivid impression, as you could tell by the way they lapped at their ice cream cones, barking between licks, or slobbered on the palms of their hands while they did their homework, which made their mothers sick, and started them thinking that it might be better to stop sending the kids to Miss Kitamura's after all before they got *really* strange, but then someone who was taking a class in folklore at the Culture Center swore she'd seen that story in one of her books, so it must be authentic, which was a comforting thought to the other mothers, one of whom said that any teacher who could get her pupils so interested in stories that weren't even in the textbooks was certainly unique, and although the word "unique" didn't sound quite right, most of them tended to agree, and there was a general sigh of relief.

Even so, since none of the mothers—either those who had grown up in the oldest part of Tokyo or the newer suburbs of Tama or Yamanote, or even those who hailed from the provinces to the north or west—ever remembered hearing a folk tale like that, some wondered whether Mitsuko Kimura hadn't spent time wandering around Southeast Asia, or maybe even as far away as Africa, which led to new speculations about her past.

"Maybe she was a hippie. They say she plays the fiddle, you know. That's probably what she was doing—riding around in the back of a caravan, playing the fiddle," said a mother in her mid-twenties, obviously mistaking "hippie" for "gypsy," but the word "hippie" suddenly reminded one of the older women of something:

"A while ago I was moving an old chest and found a weekly magazine underneath it that I hadn't seen for years—a real relic it was—and there was an advertisement in it for a natural aphrodisiac made from dried eggplants that could be ordered from something called the Hippie Shop Kitamura. You don't suppose that was Miss Kitamura?" And so the rumors grew broader and deeper, and when another mother mentioned having seen a face that looked exactly like Mitsuko's on a wanted poster for a group of terrorists at the airport, some began to imagine that she'd been in hiding all these years, but then someone else assured them that she was just an ordinary teacher who'd been running the same kind of school in the Kansai area until she came here, which was enough to satisfy some of them.

One thing everybody knew for a fact was that Mitsuko Kitamura was thirty-nine, because every child knew how much fun it was to embarrass a woman teacher by asking her age, and that this was a bit of information that would never fail to interest their mothers, so when Miss Kitamura promptly told them "Thirty-nine" in answer to their questions, they duly reported it when they went home, which was why everyone at least knew that much about her, even though none of them had the faintest idea what she'd been doing until she suddenly moved into that house just a few years ago, when a family of farmers who had lived in the area for generations sold some land to build themselves a condominium near the station, and were about to tear down their old residence when Mitsuko Kitamura, wearing a white dress, appeared out of nowhere on a mountain bike and, claiming to be an old friend of one of their relations, asked if she could rent the house for ten years. Soon after this request was granted, she opened up her school, but to the folks around there it seemed pretty strange that such a stubborn old cuss as that farmer should give in so easily to a woman who came from god knows where, so for a while there was talk about her being a mistress he'd had stashed away; but when the locals actually saw her, she didn't look the type at all, dressed in shabby farming trousers with stylish sunglasses, and after seeing her sitting under the cherry tree happily reading a novel in Polish, no one could tell what kind of family she came from, and besides, when a woman doesn't have any children, the age of thirty-nine—past youth yet not quite over the hill—makes it hard to know what category to put her in, so eventually people thereabouts got tired of gossiping and decided to leave her alone, which just goes to show that the farming community wasn't nearly as keen on rumor-mongering as the housewives in the apartment complex.

The town where all this happened was made up of two distinct areas to the north and south: in the north were the modern housing developments that had sprung up along the railway with the station at its hub, while the southern district that lined the Tama River had prospered since ancient times, and yet many people in the Tama region didn't even know it existed, even though the public housing complexes that drew people to the north had only been in existence for about thirty years, whereas the south was *really* old, with the remains of ancient pit houses discovered near the river—human dwellings that dated back farther than you could imagine—and a traditional rice-growing culture that the farmers had kept alive until the introduction of cadmium rice in the 1960s, not to mention an old stone marker carved with the words "Eight *ri* from Nihonbashi" to show where a hamlet with a cluster of inns for travelers along the Old Tokaido Road had once flourished. Until the Kitamura School opened, the youngsters from the new apartment complex had seldom visited the southern area, with all its old houses that had survived the bombing in the war, except for the occasional sketching competition or science excursion to observe frogs, but nowadays, as though escaping the herds of people at home, they would hurry toward the Tama River on the appointed day, cross the highway, pass by the grounds of the local shrine, cut quietly across a plum grove, slip through the gap in the fence around Mitsuko's house and pop up in her garden, where the first to arrive would find Miss Kitamura, not sitting at her desk waiting for them, but calmly sewing on a button, reading a book, or cutting her toenails.

One day when three second-grade girls came proudly showing off a praying mantis they'd caught on the way, Mitsuko was kneeling on the tatami wearing a threadbare pink tank top with what looked like brown rags on her bare shoulders, and when they asked: "What's that, Miss?" she calmly answered: "It's a plaster I made out of chicken shit." Ignoring the chorus of "Oh, yuck! Gross!" she went on, "Last night at Ueno Station I ran into a old friend, and while we were talking I realized what a bastard he'd turned into since I'd seen him last, and I got so fed up and depressed that my shoulders are stiff today, and chicken shit's the only thing that'll loosen them up."

The girls came closer, squealing in horror at the first whiff of the stuff, but they soon got used to it, their interest now shifting to the peach-colored tank top, about which they said quite openly, "You'd better buy a new one, Miss. That one's all raggedy," to which Mitsuko replied, as though everybody wore their clothes for as long as she did: "Oh? But it's only been seven years since I bought it."

The girls went crazy at first, clapping and jumping up and down as they chanted, "Raggedy! Raggedy!" but before long their attention turned to the breasts that were visible through the thin pink material. "The boys'll be here soon, Miss. What're you going to do then?" they said.

Laughing, Mitsuko slipped the strap of the tank top off her right shoulder and, taking her ample breast out to show them, answered: "Here's what I'll do."

Though they all shrieked "Oooh! Nasty!" it wasn't often they got a thrill like this, and when they begged her to do it again, she gave them two encores, but refused the third time, saying: "If you like to look at boobs that much, why don't you ask your mothers to show you theirs?" But then the girl who was thought to be the shyest of the three went right up to Mitsuko and pulled down both her straps, and just as the breasts came popping out like blowfish to a rousing cheer from the other two, the boys arrived.

Oddly enough, perhaps, far from sharing the girls' delight, the lads took one look and beat a hasty retreat through the hole in the fence; though they always seemed to get a kick out of watching girls cringe and squeal, *that* sort of female behavior was unsettling, and besides, they felt let down somehow to discover their teacher had such big breasts, so there they were, moping behind the fence, when Miss Kitamura, dressed in a proper blouse, came out to get them, took them by the hand, and led them back to the veranda, where there was no sign of either the pink tank top or the smelly plaster, and the little desks and chairs were neatly lined up as usual.

One day there was a new pupil at the Kitamura School, a third-grader named Fukiko. For some reason, the boys never passed her desk without smearing snot on her notebook, which was apparently what they always did at school, too. This neither angered Fukiko nor made her cry. The other girls never spoke to her or even glanced in her direction, so perhaps they failed to notice, or were pretending not to. That first day, Miss Kitamura just stared vaguely into space with big, watery eyes which, either because of nearsightedness or lack of sleep, didn't seem to focus on anything for the first hour of class until one of the boys smeared some snot on Fukiko's notebook for the third time, when she suddenly went over, grabbed his arm, and dragged him to the cabinet, giving him such a shock that he must have thought she was going to hit him, for he pulled his neck in between his shoulders and closed his eyes, but when he cautiously opened them again, Mitsuko had taken out a blue notebook with a picture of a fox on the cover, and, handing it to the boy, who stood there stiff as a board, said:

"You should wipe your snot on your own notebook. But then you wouldn't be able to read what you'd written, so use this instead."

The other kids sat there in a daze, watching, but as soon as the principle of the "snot book" began to sink in they were all clamoring for one of their own, and since there was only one left in Mitsuko's cabinet, it was decided that the rest would get theirs the following week, so the ruckus finally quieted down.

After class the following week, five girls were squatting in a circle in the garden staring at the ground, so engrossed they'd apparently forgotten to go home, and when Mitsuko, wondering what was up, went over to join them, she discovered they were watching ten ants drag a dead mayfly into their nest, having a terrible time since the entrance was too small, which was when she noticed Fukiko walking away without even stopping to see what the others were doing.

"Why don't you girls ever talk to Fukiko?" she asked.

Although none of them seemed to understand the question at first, one finally spoke up, as if she'd suddenly remembered the word she was trying to think of.

"Because she's strange."

"What's strange about her?" Mitsuko asked again.

And another piped up: "Well, she never washes her hair, and sometimes she doesn't even wear socks."

That was enough to get the rest going.

"She's fat."

"And she has a Snoopy pencil case but it's a fake."

"And she can't play dodgeball."

"And they say her father's weird."

"Oh, yeah, he hangs around in Game Centers and stuff like that."

After listening for a while, lost in thought,

Mitsuko suddenly ran back into the house and retreated behind the sliding doors, slamming them behind her.

One August day soon after school had let out for the summer, a man of twenty-seven or -eight came calling at the Kitamura School with an old-fashioned leather suitcase but not a trace of sweat on him despite the hot sun beating down from above, and although he didn't look like a friend of Mitsuko's, with his closely cropped hair, immaculate white shirt, neatly creased trousers and polished leather shoes, he seemed to know all about her house, for he walked straight into the garden through the gap in the fence, and when he saw Mitsuko repairing her mountain bike, half-naked, her hair disheveled, he went right up to her and said:

"I'm here to stay."

Mitsuko's eyes widened and rolled upward, her mouth dropped open and she forgot to close it, and since she couldn't think what to say, she kept touching her throat with her fingertips, while the man silently put his suitcase down on the veranda, took off his wristwatch, and gave it two or three hard shakes as though to get the water out of it.

"Did you get my telegram?" he asked with a knowing laugh.

Unable to take in what was happening, Mitsuko stared blankly up at him and shook her head, furrowing her brow as though trying to think, so the man introduced himself in an even clearer tone:

"You can call me Taro. Under the circumstances, it mightn't be advisable to use my real name, but I can't think of any other."

Still in a daze, Mitsuko nodded weakly, and then,

as though he'd suddenly thought of something, the man took her by the hand and, like a host inviting her into his own home, escorted her to the veranda, where he removed those fine leather shoes with a single shake of each ankle, without even bothering to stoop to untie them, before stepping up onto the wooden floor, and the strangest thing was that even so, when Mitsuko looked down, she saw the shoes neatly lined up on the stone below. He then took Mitsuko's waist in his large palms, which were neither hot nor cold nor the least bit sweaty, and lightly lifted her.

"Did you get my telegram?" he asked again.

This time Mitsuko hurriedly shook her head, whereupon the man slipped off her shorts as easily as drawing a handkerchief out of his sleeve, laid her on her back, and very politely, still in his shirt and pants, fitted his body on top of hers, then, gently pressing his canine teeth against the delicate skin of her neck, began sucking noisily, with Mitsuko's face growing paler all the while until she suddenly flushed crimson and the beads of sweat standing out on her forehead got sticky from the shock of feeling a thing with both the flexibility and indifference of a vegetable slide into her vagina, but as she writhed, struggling to get away, he flipped her over and, easily grabbing her thighs, one in each hand, raised them up and began licking her rectum, now poised precariously in midair. The sheer size of his tongue, the amount of saliva dripping from it, and the heavy panting were all literally extraordinary; and besides, even in this sweltering heat, the huge hands that gripped Mitsuko's thighs neither trembled nor grew the least bit moist no matter how long they held her that way, and when at last he gently pulled her up into a sitting position, the dark eyes that gazed into hers were tranquil, without so much as a droplet of sweat on the forehead or nose, and since his hair was as neat as ever, she reached out without thinking and touched it, only to find it as coarse as the bristles of a scrubbing brush, the skin beneath as smooth and strong as cowhide, and while she sat there as though in a trance, stroking his head, the man quietly, seriously, returned her gaze, until on a sudden impulse, leaving Mitsuko still naked from the waist down, he ran into the kitchen and started stir-frying some bean sprouts.

When she finally came to herself, Mitsuko put her shorts back on and went into the kitchen to find a meal ready, the table neatly set with plates and bowls for rice and soup, all looking like dolls' dishes in the man's big hands. He'd been sitting there waiting for her, and at the sight of her let out a cheer, then tucked into the rice in a manner that was somehow refined but frighteningly energetic, wolfing it down so fast that his bowl was empty before Mitsuko had even picked up her chopsticks, then quickly helping himself to a second bowlful, which he devoured in no time, and when she gave him a reproachful look, he licked the bowl clean with his long tongue, then suddenly stood up and, taking a rag from the suitcase he'd left on the veranda, rinsed it, wrung it out at the kitchen sink, and began scrubbing the wooden corridor. As Mitsuko's eyes moved back and forth between her rice bowl, still more than half full, and the man washing the floor, with the muscles in his bottom pumping up and down in perfect rhythm as he pushed the rag along on all fours, he looked so funny she burst out laughing, and as she giggled and ate, the floorboards began to give off a dull sheen, and by the time she finished he'd taken a duster from the suitcase and begun dusting the rooms inside, easily reaching corners so high up that Mitsuko would have had to stand on a chair to get to them, scooping up cobwebs in his hands as they fluttered down and gobbling them like cotton candy, and though for a while she sat there motionless among the motes of dust, sparkling in the western sunlight, when she saw him take out a blue fold-up broom and start sweeping the tatami, she went out into the garden where she wouldn't be in his way, and was gazing at the bike she'd been repairing earlier, standing there with a tube dangling wantonly from the tire like an intestine, when she heard someone greet her:

"Good afternoon, Miss." She looked up in surprise to see two of her pupils standing on the other side of the fence in red swimming trunks.

"Who's that man, Miss?" they asked bluntly.

Not knowing how to answer, Mitsuko tried to gloss over it with a simple, "Oh, just somebody I know," which didn't satisfy the children.

"Why's he cleaning your house?" they wanted to know, but as Mitsuko was fumbling for another reply, luckily they heard the distant voice of another child calling, and raced off in that direction.

Not that the two boys forgot what they'd seen— far from it; in fact, when one of them got home he ran up the apartment steps two at a time, and without stopping to catch his breath or call out "I'm home!" went straight to his mother with the news.

"When we went by Miss Kitamura's on the way home from the pool, a man was cleaning her house."

"A man? What kind of man?"

He didn't know, really, but finally managed to say: "Like Superman, sort of. Real big and kind of scary."

"About how old was he?"

"Around twenty, or maybe thirty, I guess."

His mother laughed, thinking some nephew of Miss Kitamura's must have come up to Tokyo and found the house so dirty he decided to do something about it; people might say young men were turning into sissies these days, but you had to admire a man who liked a clean house.

"What do you think—would a young unmarried man nowadays go so far as to clean a single woman's house for her?" she asked when she ran into another mother from the next building and told her all about it, but the other woman cocked her head and said:

"A nephew? I wonder. Seems more likely City Hall has sent in a social worker. A place with that many children running in and out has to be sanitary, you know."

As the two women talked, a certain suspicion did, admittedly, arise in their minds, but it was left unsaid, until several days later the same child reported seeing the man again when he'd passed Miss Kitamura's place on the way home from the pool that evening; this time he was in the garden "cutting the grass," which didn't sound right at all, and even though the Kitamura School was out for the summer, Mitsuko's name was soon on mothers' lips throughout the apartment complex, along with the phrase "cutting the grass," which took on a special meaning, though no one could have told you exactly what it was, and although Mitsuko herself didn't know the content of the rumors, she was sure there were plenty floating around, since the man she was now used to calling "Taro" had been seen by the same pupil twice in a row, and it wasn't just a matter of "having been seen," either, for while the first time he'd just been cleaning the house, which was all right, on the second occasion he'd been sitting in the grass about to tickle her rectum with a bunch of clover when the boy's face had appeared through the fence, startling Mitsuko, who was lying face down but now sat up, burying her legs in the grass and yanking her skirt down, while Taro, apparently not noticing the child, tried to lift up the hem she'd just pulled down, and then, still oblivious to the boy staring at them with ever widening eyes, picked her up and planted her firmly between the branches of the cherry tree.

If his physical strength was somewhat out of the

ordinary, so was the rhythm of his days, for while the sun was out he'd lie around sleeping, but at six in the evening he'd be up cleaning the house and making a sumptuous meal, and by the time he and Mitsuko were finished eating, he would suddenly be full of energy; ready for lovemaking, after which he always went out alone into the darkness to spend half the night running around god knows where, only returning—without a sound—just as Mitsuko was about to go to sleep, but since Taro then kept her up until dawn with his lovemaking again, Mitsuko could no longer get up in the morning and would be dozing off all day, except when some salesman marched into the garden unannounced and she'd have to get up in a hurry, but unlike Taro, who was always alert the minute he awoke, with his eyes wide open and his hair as neat as if he'd just combed it, Mitsuko would emerge bleary-eyed, her hair sticking out in all directions, so that the person outside the door would blurt out: "Sorry. Seems I've caught you at a bad time," at which Mitsuko would blush, not knowing how to explain, and while she was busy making lame excuses, the woman who ran the general store in the neighborhood was telling everyone she met that Mitsuko Kitamura had "got herself a man," an odd phrase that the housewives from the apartment complex refrained from using because they found it rather crude, but when they tried something lighter like "Miss Kitamura has a boyfriend," it sounded like a joke, so for lack of anything better they ended up saying, "It seems there's a young man living at Miss Kitamura's," which you could take to mean anything you chose, and though they were all dying to see this young man for themselves, during the summer vacation the housewives had no reason to venture into the southern part of town, so they sent their children to the pool, reminding them to be sure to stop by Miss Kitamura's to say hello on the way back, sometimes even sending along some sweets for her, but these kids, though they looked the picture of innocence, were actually just as keen to see Taro themselves, for the very sight of him gave them that thrill children get from seeing something they're not supposed to, and even if they didn't catch Mitsuko doing anything in particular, even if Taro was just sitting on a stone in a corner of the garden staring blankly into space, their hearts beat faster, and some didn't so much drop in to see Miss Kitamura on the way home from the pool as go swimming just so they could catch a glimpse of Taro.

Taro didn't mind the children staring at him in

the least. Although he got nervous when dogs or cats wandered into the garden, people he simply ignored, which worried Mitsuko, who found herself wondering one day what would happen after August when classes started again, for the Kitamura School was her only source of income. Though half asleep, she was still pursuing this thought when she looked at the clock and saw it was already past five, so she sat up and glanced around the room to discover that Taro, who had appeared out of nowhere, was right in front of her, burying his head between her knees, to smell her, she assumed, as she could tell by the sound that he was breathing through his nose, and he went on doing this until her legs started to go numb and she shifted to one side and tried to stand up, which was difficult, of course, with Taro clinging to her like that, holding on so long in fact that

Mitsuko thought she'd go out of her mind, but she knew that he never got tired of sniffing an odor he liked. Although he didn't have a job—didn't do anything, really, except take care of the laundry, cooking, and cleaning—he was never bored enough to resort to reading or watching television, and his principal hobby was smelling her body; when he got started he could sometimes keep at it for an hour or more, which at first bored Mitsuko to tears, but in time made her realize that her body was always slightly damp with perspiration and that, far from being odorless, her sweat carried various faint but distinct aromas not unlike those of seaweed, shellfish, citrus fruit, milk, and iron, depending on minor shifts in mood, so that when she was surprised by something, for instance, she'd notice a certain odor in the air around her and think, "Ah. I must be surprised," which is how she got into the habit of smelling herself as she reacted to things.

Oddly enough, Taro wasn't at all attracted to breasts, and never touched Mitsuko's; although kissing didn't interest him either, sucking certainly did, but the spot he always chose for that was Mitsuko's neck, which he'd attack like a vampire, leaving a number of reddish-purple, dough-nut-shaped marks, which Mitsuko would have to hide, in spite of the heat, by wrapping an Indian cotton scarf around her neck, making her sweat all the more; and when she caught sight of herself in a mirror and saw how red and swollen her face was, with dry lips and a rounder nose than before, she realized she'd never seen herself looking this bad—all because of Taro, which seemed strange, but perhaps having someone so strongly attached to you did actually ruin your looks, and besides, he never looked her up and down in the coolly appraising way that other people did anyway, while Mitsuko, who at one time hadn't minded being appraised like that, now had him always grabbing her and holding on for dear life, which left her no time to repair the damage.

One day a group of seven or eight third-graders dropped by with their mothers on the way back from an outing, to bring her a watermelon, so Mitsuko busied herself pouring iced barley tea and setting out cushions, glancing nervously around the room all the while, even though everything, thanks to Taro, looked neat enough and the tea glasses sparkled like crystal, so to anyone ignorant of the circumstances there would have seemed no need to worry, but Mitsuko didn't know what she'd do if Taro, who was asleep in the next room, were suddenly to get up; on top of which, these proper-looking housewives seemed to have brought an invasion of odors with them, waves of sweat, perfume, the paste they use for pickling vegetables, detergent, blood, tooth powder, insecticide, coffee, fish, cough medicine, Band-Aids, and nylons, which confused her completely, making it impossible to distinguish the subtle aroma that hovered around her own body, without which she couldn't be sure how she was feeling, so although it was only natural that she should be annoyed with these people for bursting in on her with no warning, without the smell to prove it her own feelings didn't seem real to her, which upset her all the more. As Mitsuko joined halfheartedly in the conversation, taking care not to breathe through her nose, wishing they would all leave soon, the clock on the wall struck six, and at that very moment the sliding doors opened and Taro appeared.

He was wearing nothing but a cotton summer kimono, which opened at the front when he put his right leg forward, but while the mothers, of course, pretended they hadn't seen a thing, one of the kids cried out "Wow! Awesome!"—though it wasn't altogether clear what he was referring to.

There was no reaction from Taro, so perhaps he hadn't heard, but one of the mothers whispered "Oh my god, it's Iinuma," then promptly clammed up, which sounded ominous to Mitsuko, yet no one else apparently had noticed, for they all started saying things like, "We've been making such a nuisance of ourselves. We'd better be running along now," as if they knew it was about time for Taro to begin his nightly routine, and although Mitsuko had intended to be polite and ask them to stay a little longer, she accidentally bit her tongue and missed her chance, so with Taro just standing there without so much as saying hello, an awkward silence ensued, until the women, shooting disapproving looks at this rude young man who still refused to speak, stood up and started dithering about, preparing to leave, while a Mrs. Orita, the person who had whispered "Oh my god, it's Iinuma," watched a fly buzzing around her as though it were a bee, following it with frightened eyes straight out the door ahead of all the rest, apparently only too happy to get away.

After seeing them off, Mitsuko stood vacantly in the doorway for a while, but at the sound of Taro washing the glasses in the kitchen, she stirred herself and got a fan, which she began waving wildly about, trying to chase out all the intrusive smells, occasionally stopping to think, then fanning again, repeating the pattern over and over again.

After having sex with Mitsuko as usual, Taro went out, and a while later the phone rang. It was Mrs. Orita.

"I didn't get a chance to talk at your house with so many people around, but it's about that young man who's living with you; I just saw him for the first time today, but he looks so much like a fellow called Iinuma who used to work under my husband that I couldn't help wondering.... He was one of my husband's favorites, you see, but he disappeared three years ago, and his wife's been looking for him ever since, poor thing, so if that really is Iinuma, I'd like her to know."

At first Mitsuko answered coldly, "Yes ... yes," but as she listened the air seemed to close in on her and she found it hard to speak, so when the woman said, "I'm going to talk to Iinuma's wife and have her go see for herself," as though it were already decided, she couldn't object.

When Mrs. Orita asked, 'Where did you meet that young man, anyway?" she fudged it, since telling what had really happened was out of the question.

"Oh, just by chance; someone introduced him, and asked me to rent him a room. But tell me, how do you write 'Iinuma'?"

Ignoring her question, Mrs. Orita proceeded to explain at great length what sort of person he was, so Mitsuko protested:

"But I'm not very interested in his character— sorry, it may seem odd, but I don't really want to hear about it." And she started to put the phone down, then reluctantly picked it up again and, to help her endure the steady stream of chatter pouring into her ear, held her head in her left hand and closed her eyes, patiently waiting for it to end.

According to Mrs. Orita, Taro Iinuma had gone to work for the pharmaceutical company her husband was with after graduating from a university in Tokyo, and though her husband had taken a liking to him from the start, if you'd asked him why, he wouldn't have been able to tell you, but if forced to give a reason he would have said it was because young Iinuma was the kind of guy who could accept your point of view—could say, "I see what you mean," without sounding snide or insincere in any way. For example, one day not long after he'd joined the company, Orita had seen him in the parking lot leaning against a car with one shoe off, wiping the sole with a handkerchief embroidered with violets, and when he'd asked him what he was doing, Iinuma had said: "I stepped on a worm and got my shoe all dirty." Looking at the expanse of gray asphalt, Orita had shouted, "How could there be worms in a place like this!" to which Iinuma had replied: "I see what you mean," and stopped wiping right then and there. Afterward, though, when he was telling his wife about it, Orita had said he now realized that Iinuma had probably stepped in a pile of dog shit but for some reason couldn't come out and say it, and that was why the poor fellow had lied.

Poor Iinuma—he was often the butt of his coworkers' jokes, too. For example, the year he joined, he never used company pencils but always brought his own with him, like an elementary school kid, and no matter how many times he was asked about it, he refused to say why, so they all started teasing him, saying things like: "He'll only use pencils with Miss Kitty on them." Orita had taken him drinking and, when he'd loosened up a bit, asked him about it, too, first assuring him that he didn't have to talk about it unless he really wanted to, so, on condition that Orita promise not to tell anyone else, Iinuma had explained his behavior to him: the "reason," it seemed, was that the girl who sat across from him had the habit of chewing on her pencils when no one was looking, and since she was always leaving them around, she often came to borrow one from Iinuma, but that wasn't all—she'd sometimes leave pencils on Iinuma's desk in return for the ones he'd lent her, and since company pencils were all the same, there was always the possibility he might use one that she had chewed on, and the very thought of it made his palms itch.

"I envy you, getting pencils a pretty girl's chewed on," Orita had said, trying to make a joke of it. "Do they still have her spit and tooth marks on them?" But far from relaxing, Iinuma had stiffened noticeably, which made Orita realize that since kidding wouldn't work, he'd have to give it to him straight. "You'll never get anywhere if you let little things like that bother you. You've got to stop being so nervous," he told him, and Iinuma had replied, in that special way of his, "I see what you mean," and stopped bringing his own pencils to work the very next day, much to Orita's relief, but while he'd felt pleased with himself for having given such good advice and even more well-disposed toward Iinuma for taking it, there had been various other incidents after that, such as the time he noticed that whenever Iinuma sat down he shifted his bottom this way and that on the seat of the chair, and no matter how hard his colleagues tried not to laugh, they couldn't help exchanging winks and snickers, until Orita decided to do something about it, and told Iinuma about a doctor he'd once seen for his hemorrhoids, but Iinuma had said that wasn't the problem: no, he didn't have hemorrhoids, it was just that his skin was so delicate that when he used the toilet seats in the company men's room, he broke out in a rash, and since Orita didn't know what to do, he spoke to his wife, who told him there was something you could buy to put over a toilet seat—a plastic bag, shaped like a long sock—and when he suggested that Iinuma try it, he'd looked surprised and said, "I see what you mean," then went out and bought one of them, and started using it.

Four years earlier, Iinuma had been engaged to Ryoko, a thin, soft-spoken woman who looked a bit like a fox; she worked in the same section, and since she was four years younger and only a high school graduate, Orita had felt confident she wouldn't frighten even a timid man like Iinuma, but still wasn't sure how the young man felt about his coming marriage, for he had the impression that although Ryoko was happy enough, Iinuma wasn't so enthusiastic, and he wondered if Ryoko had found out about some weakness of Iinuma's, making him feel obliged to marry her even though there was someone else he liked better, which was a bit worrying, so he'd asked him about it in a roundabout way, and since it had seemed that wasn't the case, he'd let it go, but though the wedding had gone off without a hitch and nothing noteworthy had happened afterward, about a year later, without a word of warning either to Ryoko or the company, Iinuma had suddenly disappeared.

It wasn't as though he hadn't had a chance to talk to Iinuma alone after the marriage, but they'd been busy at work that year, and the two or three times they'd gone drinking Iinuma hadn't had much to say; in fact, he had only mentioned Ryoko once, when Orita remembered asking: "How's Ryoko? Bet she's a good wife." Looking as though he really didn't want to say it, Iinuma had replied: "Sometimes when I get home, I find my toothbrush has been broken into little bits. It's surprising how strong even small women are, isn't it?" Not knowing how to answer but thinking he should at least try to be encouraging, Orita had said, "Sounds like a woman you can depend on," but Iinuma had just hung his head, and when he spoke again it was to ask: "Mr. Orita, do you like miso soup with fried bean curd? They say foxes do, but I don't," which made the older man say sternly,

"Look, if she's always fixing something you don't like, why don't you tell her about it? There's no reason to put up with it," but Iinuma had mumbled, "No, well, actually she doesn't make that soup, it's just that ..." The words then trailed off, leaving Orita patiently waiting for him to continue: "... it *smells* like she does. I don't like smells of any kind, and I can't stand sleeping closed up in a little room with another animal, even a hamster. You can hear them breathing, you know. And the rhythm is completely different from mine, so just listening to it makes me feel like I'm suffocating."

This, to Mitsuko's relief, was enough to convince her that the man Mrs. Orita was talking about was definitely not her Taro, who loved smells so much he couldn't live without them.

"All right, then, please tell Ryoko she's welcome

to come over any time and see if this guy's her husband," she said into the phone, and despite an obvious disappointment at hearing Mitsuko sound so cool and reasonable about it, Mrs. Orita called Ryoko immediately, explained how to get to the house, and strongly recommended that she go, only to find that Ryoko, too, was perfectly calm, asking, "Does Miss Kitamura like fruit? What do you think I should take her?" which wasn't at all the sort of thing Mrs. Orita had expected her to be worried about, so she hung up feeling rather put out.

It was an evening late in August when Ryoko went to see Mitsuko Kitamura: the sky was heavy and so swollen with moisture it looked about to burst, and as the thunder rumbled like a lion growling deep in its throat and it suddenly grew dark, a small, thin figure with glittering eyes slipped into the garden through the break in the fence. Mitsuko thought it was a child at first, but closer up she saw a woman in her mid-twenties, who, after a brief glance at Taro, sitting in a corner of the garden gazing blankly at the sky, stared Mitsuko in the face as she bowed and said:

"I'm Ryoko."

Just as Mitsuko hurried her into the house, large drops began to fall, bringing Taro slowly to his feet to join them inside, and since Ryoko's expression didn't change at all when she was looking him over, Mitsuko felt reassured, concluding as she poured her guest a glass of barley tea that Iinuma the missing husband and this Taro must be two different people after all, while Ryoko now kept her eyes fixed on Mitsuko, not even glancing in Taro's direction when he stood up, went into the back room, and closed the sliding doors behind him. By now the evening shower was a downpour, but when Mitsuko got up to close the shutters Ryoko suddenly pounced on her, grabbing both ankles with a strength you wouldn't have expected of her, so that Mitsuko flipped onto her back on the tatami, and found herself staring into Ryoko's eyes, which looked so much like Taro's it shocked her. Pinning her down, Ryoko pulled the scarf from around Mitsuko's neck, sniffed at the reddish-purple, doughnut-shaped marks that were hidden beneath it, and asked in a harsh voice:

"Did you get my telegram?"

Mitsuko shook her head like a child falsely accused of something until Ryoko took her hands away, and while Mitsuko was picking herself up off the floor, she took a blue name card from her handbag and said:

"Come to my house tomorrow."

It was so obviously an order that Mitsuko, unable to say no, just sat there in a daze, watching the rain drench the veranda, and by the time the evening sun had begun to reappear between the clouds, lighting up the strands of raindrops, Ryoko was nowhere to be seen.

Now alert but still unable to move, feeling as though she were tied up, Mitsuko eventually got up and went to the back room to see what Taro was doing, only to find that he, too, was no longer there.

The next day Mitsuko went to a neighboring town to visit Ryoko, who lived in an apartment complex which, except for a reddish tinge to the outside walls, was exactly like the one where Mitsuko's pupils lived, and following the numbers in the address—1-7-6-4—she found Ryoko's apartment, climbed the stairs to arrive in front of a door identical to the ones on either side, and rang the bell, but when Ryoko appeared looking meek and mild, the glitter of last night gone from her eyes, Mitsuko had no qualms about going in, nor did anything catch her eye as she surveyed the room, which smelled of fried bean curd, except perhaps for something on top of the dresser that looked like a bit of sacred rope, the kind that's hung in Shinto shrines to ward off evil, and as her eyes wandered over it she noticed Ryoko smirking in the background.

Ryoko proceeded to inform her that the man she'd gone to check out the day before was definitely her husband, but she had not been shocked by his disappearance three years earlier, nor was she still searching for him without a clue to his current whereabouts as the Oritas believed, for she saw him occasionally in passing, and knew that recently he'd been "playing around" at night with a man called Toshio Matsubara, whom she'd also met—and who had struck her as surprisingly ordinary, though certainly not dull—but she knew her husband must also have a woman he played around with during the day, and had been wanting to meet her, too, when Mrs. Orita had obliged by creating this opportunity. All this, however, was news to Mitsuko, to whom it came as a huge shock. Toshio Matsubara was her pupil Fukiko's father, and since he'd been raising her alone since the death of her mother some years before, it was he who had brought the girl to the Kitamura School to see about enrolling her, and though he was small and stout, with a loose, flabby face that made him look as if he might burst into tears at any moment, and despite having a right canine tooth missing which made him whistle his s's in an irritating way, he'd been very polite, seeming to trust Mitsuko's judgment completely, so she had soon warmed to him, and as they chatted away like old friends, she realized that he knew about all sorts of fascinating things like the life cycle of the crocodile and the structure of Indonesian houses, and someone told her later that he was good at his job as well, so he certainly didn't seem the type to be "playing around"; but since she didn't know exactly what Ryoko had meant by the term, she asked her.

"By 'playing around,' do you mean with women?"

"No, just the two of them," Ryoko said sharply.

"What exactly do they do?"

This question sent Ryoko into spasms of laughter, making all further inquiry impossible, so Mitsuko waited quietly until Ryoko started again on her disturbing monologue:

"That man is no longer the Taro Iinuma I married. My husband was a nervous, wishy-washy sort of person, who couldn't stand the touch of somebody else's skin, and who I'm sure I would have divorced long ago anyway, but though he apparently still likes to keep things tidy, the Taro I saw yesterday is a completely different person. There was an incident just before he disappeared that may have accounted for the change in him. Anyway, even though Taro's stopped being the man I was married to, there are one or two things about him that are still the same, so I thought if I decided to go back to him, I'd have to make myself physically as strong as he is now, which is why I started going to a dojo, but then as I got into training I found I was far more interested in that than in getting my husband back."

Still slightly bewildered, Mitsuko asked: "When

you say 'training,' you mean something like aikido?"

In the twinkling of an eye, Ryoko picked her up and laid her flat across the table, and while Mitsuko was flailing her legs and arms about, struggling to get down, she banged her knee against the wall, but hardly had time to yell "Ouch!" before Ryoko had her mouth on the spot, sucking at it like an octopus with loud smacking sounds until she'd drawn the pain right out.

"I feel I'm gradually turning into Taro somehow," Ryoko said, which made Mitsuko blush, and as she rubbed her knee, Ryoko told her about the incident three years earlier that may have been the catalyst for Taro's transformation.

On top of a nearby hill that wasn't yet covered with rows of new houses, a restaurant had just opened, and one Sunday afternoon Taro and Ryoko had tea and cheesecake there, and after buying a steak and some sauce to take home, they started down the hill behind the restaurant, thinking it might be nice to walk to the station, and as they strolled along the lonely path through the woods they thought they heard an odd noise behind them, like the rumble of an engine, but when they turned around there was nothing there, just some old pipes stacked up in a clearing where some trees had been chopped down, so they went on, turning onto a narrow road, where they heard the same rumbling sound, this time coming from the waist-high grass growing in the fields on either side of them, and just as Ryoko muttered "I wonder what that is?" some dogs leapt out at them, one after another, but seeing they weren't very big, only about the size of Shibas, Ryoko wasn't frightened at first—even though thoughts like "They're not wearing collars, so they must be strays," and "They're growling" did cross her mind—until one of the dogs jumped on Taro, and the moment he screamed, the others followed suit (except for one that went after the bag with the steak which he threw away as far as he could), sinking their teeth into his legs, refusing to let go, tearing his trousers to shreds as he yelled, "Stop it! Let me go! You're getting me all dirty!" Ryoko ran back to the phone booth they'd passed to call the police, and waited there until some men from City Hall came with sticks and nets, but when she led them to the spot, the dogs had vanished, leaving Taro lying unconscious by the side of the road. After rushing him to a nearby hospital in a police car, they found that he had fifteen or sixteen bite marks on his legs, none of them fortunately very deep, and since he didn't appear to have rabies and soon regained consciousness, Ryoko felt they'd been pretty lucky—a feeling that lasted only until Taro's grandmother drove up in a taxi with a wild look in her eye and some dire warnings. "The boy's lost. An evil spirit's got him now," she announced before bursting into tears, while Taro's mother, who had arrived a little later, looked embarrassed and made excuses.

"You mustn't listen to Granny. She's always been superstitious, but lately she's joined one of those crazy new religions, and you never know what kind of nonsense she's going to come out with."

For some reason, hearing this made the back of Ryoko's earlobes turn cold as ice, and, grabbing Taro, she pulled him up and shook him. "You're not going to turn weird on me now, are you?" she yelled at him.

Perhaps shocked at the way she was behaving,

Taro said nothing, which only made things worse, until all the irritation she'd been keeping in check exploded. "Why don't you say something? Have you gone dumb?" she yelled again.

From then on, Taro stopped talking altogether, which drove Ryoko to new heights of anger, but when she tried to break his silence by throwing dishes at him, he finally left home. He didn't go far, however, as she still saw him in the park or at the station, each time looking more muscular, with a brighter gleam in his eyes, moving with such agility that, more often than not, he'd be gone before she had a chance to call out to him.

Taro must have stopped going to work after that, and when Mr. Orita called to ask what had happened, she told him through her tears: "The fact is he's disappeared, and I don't know where he's gone." But it wasn't sadness that made her cry, it was because she was afraid he might wonder why she hadn't told anyone until now and start asking some nasty questions, so she'd chosen to play the role of a woman so heartbroken she didn't know what she was doing, though her real feelings toward Taro no longer involved anger but jealousy, for compared to Taro, who looked fitter every time she saw him, her own body moved so slowly and awkwardly it seemed downright un-attractive even to her, which was why she'd started "training."

In the end, Mitsuko left Ryoko's apartment without really understanding either what Taro and Toshio did when they "played around," or the nature of Ryoko's "training," but when she got home she looked at Taro and thought, so this guy used to be an ordinary wage slave, and felt the old excitement slipping away. After school started on September 1, however, the children came back, and Mitsuko was busy teaching from late afternoon on into the evening, while Taro started leaving during the day and not returning until after dark, which suited Mitsuko fine, since seeing him in broad daylight somehow disgusted her now; in the darkened house, in the middle of the night, she didn't mind, but for the rest of the time she wanted to rub him out of her life.

She developed a special fondness for Fukiko: before the vacation she'd merely wanted to protect her from all the bullying she got, but now she combed her hair and trimmed her nails, and told her to come an hour early so they could go over her schoolwork, and when Fukiko still did poorly Mitsuko got as angry as if it had been herself. Fukiko, on the other hand, seemed to find Mitsuko a little creepy, and refused to come early at first, making up stories about things she had to do, and hurrying home after class before Mitsuko had a chance to speak to her, as though she didn't want all this attention; so when Mitsuko cornered her one day and asked, "What do you do about dinner?" she just said, "My father gives me money," which didn't satisfy Mitsuko, who asked again, "And what do you spend it on?" Mitsuko's exasperated sigh when she heard the answer—"Yakitori, or cheeseburgers"—made the girl feel so embarrassed she burst into tears, so Mitsuko told her, "Starting tomorrow you'll eat with me," which didn't particularly please her but left her with little choice, making her decide to start crying again, except now she couldn't stop; and as Mitsuko wiped away her tears, her resistance seemed to crumble and she buried her face in Mitsuko's bosom and cried her heart out, and since even her father, who didn't like people and warned her to stay away from them, never had a bad word to say about this woman, it didn't seem like such a bad thing to do.

So Fukiko forgot herself from time to time and began to depend on her. Every day after school, she would go over to Mitsuko's place, eat the dinner Taro made, and after he'd gone out, except for Thursdays when she had a class there with the other third-graders, either go outdoors to play or shut herself in the back room, until about five minutes before Taro was due home when, almost instinctively, she would leave. She was soon accustomed to this routine, and if she never smiled when she saw Mitsuko, she no longer ran away from her, while Mitsuko tried to draw her out by buying her books, but Fukiko hated books, and didn't really care for food, either, unless it was flavored with ketchup or mayonnaise, dawdling over the meals Taro cooked but feeling duty-bound to eat them, casting sly, sidelong glances at the cook himself, who seemed to fascinate her.

Fukiko wasn't a talkative child, but when asked a question, perhaps because she didn't really understand what the other person wanted to know, she'd sometimes go on about unrelated topics, such as the time Mitsuko said: "Your father knows about a lot of things, doesn't he? Once when he came here, he told me all about crocodiles. I bet he's been to lots of different countries."

Fukiko thought for a moment before replying, looking rather pleased with herself: "Dad's always saying he wants to go somewhere, but he just packs a suitcase and puts it by the bathroom door, and never goes anywhere. He says the last time he went on a trip was before he got the job he has now."

Mitsuko tried again: "He must be busy working," but Fukiko just cocked her head, without so much as a nod, and it occurred to Mitsuko that she'd never heard Fukiko use the word "busy," which was unusual for a child nowadays—she'd found that odd from the start.

Another time, when Mitsuko asked, "What does your father say about Taro?" Fukiko just gave her a dubious look and said, "Has he met Taro?" and since she could tell by the look in the eyes gazing up at her that the girl wasn't playing dumb, Mitsuko regretted having asked her in the first place.

You couldn't say Fukiko looked clever, gripping her chopsticks with her sticky fingers, pulling at her ears, or just sitting there, lost in thought as she slowly put her food in her mouth, and yet, watching her, Mitsuko often felt a love akin to irritation well up in her, so strong it hurt, and sometimes she even wished Taro would hurry up and leave so the two of them could be alone, not that they did anything special together; in fact, more often than not they'd end up quarreling, because Mitsuko would be determined to read to her, and Fukiko wanted no part of it, but when, for example, Mitsuko took Fukiko's blouse off so she could sew on the buttons that were hanging by a thread, the girl would sit there beside her, naked to the waist, intently watching the movements of her fingers, and after a while her head would be leaning against Mitsuko's shoulder, and when Mitsuko was sure she must have fallen asleep, she'd look over to find the child still gravely following the needle with her eyes, so Mitsuko would say:

"You like sewing on buttons better than reading, don't you?"

"That's because I'm not 'smart' like you."

This cheeky sort of remark only made Mitsuko angry again.

After she took the girl under her wing, the other kids stopped bullying her openly, but there were more nasty rumors going the rounds than ever before, especially one about Fukiko's father "swinging his hips" at the Game Center; this was an expression the junior high school boys used to refer to various things, but it had filtered down to the elementary school children, who were all using it now without knowing what it meant, and though it upset their mothers to overhear this sort of language, they didn't understand it either, and had no one to ask. When Mitsuko first heard it from

Mrs. Orita, for some reason it cracked her up, not that *she* knew what it meant herself, it just sounded so funny, but Mrs. Orita frowned as though she thought she was laughing at her.

"Don't you think it needs looking into, though? After all, there's AIDS to worry about, too, you know."

Unable to see what she was getting at, Mitsuko blurted out: "Look into? What's there to look into?"

Mrs. Orita was quite fed up by now with Mitsuko, who had never once said anything that made sense to her, and in total exasperation started to say: "But don't you see? Your Taro—if ...," then realized that since Taro didn't belong to Miss Kitamura, "your" was hardly appropriate, and that she was under no obligation to investigate the company he kept, either.

Beginning at last to catch on, Mitsuko said: "Oh, if that's what it is, there's nothing to worry about," meaning that since she wasn't sleeping with Taro any more, it made no difference to her what he did or with whom. But Mrs. Orita, who didn't have that sort of thing in mind at all, inquired disapprovingly:

"Hadn't you better sit down, the two of you, and have a good talk about this? Of course the best thing would be for Iinuma to go back to Ryoko, but if neither of them wants to start over again, Iinuma could divorce Ryoko, and then he'd be free to marry *you*, which seems a logical thing to do. Either way, doesn't it bother you to have him hanging around in gay bars?..."

Mitsuko started at the words "marry" and "gay bar," as it dawned on her that maybe the Game Centers the kids were always talking about were actually places gays went to, and she was the only one who didn't know. Even if that *were* the case, though, Taro's behavior no longer had much to do with her, so she replied:

"But what's wrong with that? There's nothing I can do about it anyway. And why on earth should he have to marry me?"

Mrs. Orita blinked. "Just what do you think he is—you and Ryoko both? Poor Iinuma! It isn't fair!" There were tears in her eyes when she left for home.

One weekend toward the end of September, the Oritas took their son to Mrs. Orita's parents' for a visit, and when they got off the train at Ueno Station on Sunday night, the boy squatted down on the platform, saying his gym shoelaces had got tangled up, which, as his mother soon saw, was indeed the case, with his left and right shoes actually tied together in a terrific knot, and while she was standing there waiting for him to sort out the mess and retie the laces properly, wondering how in the world things like this happened, she glanced over at the opposite platform, where she saw Taro Iinuma and Toshio Matsubara, each holding a suitcase, standing so close together their bodies touched, so she grabbed her husband by the arm, and though he stood there gawking around for a bit, he finally saw them too.

"Iinuma!" he called out.

Taro quickly spotted Mr. Orita and bowed politely, not the least bit flustered, and when Orita yelled, "Where're you going?" he answered in a clear, carrying voice: "Thank you for all your help."

Orita's "You idiot!" was drowned out by the

express train coming in, hiding the two behind it. Leaving the luggage with his wife, Orita ran down the stairs and across to the other platform, but soon returned, out of breath, gasping:

"They got away. Let's call the police."

It was just as well his wife stopped him, for as even he soon realized, there was nothing criminal about their going on a trip together somewhere. What his wife said made much better sense.

"We've got to let Miss Kitamura know."

But when they called Mitsuko from the plat-form, no one answered the phone, so there was nothing to do but go home, where they tried again, but still with no result, which seemed very strange considering it was already the middle of the night, so the Oritas, who couldn't very well just sit there, got into the car and drove down the bumpy, ill-lit roads of the southern district to

Mitsuko's house, only to find it looking dark and deserted. No matter how many times they called "Miss Kitamura!" there was no reply but, oddly, the door was unlocked, and when they opened it and went inside, turning on the lights, they found everything neatly put away, with a strange chill in the air, and then Mr. Orita gasped in surprise, pointing at a poster tied to a pillar in a spot where anyone coming through the garden could see it immediately, for written on it in big letters with a pink magic marker were the words "The Kitamura School is now closed."

The next day, the Oritas got a telegram from Mitsuko, saying: HAVE ESCAPED WITH FUKIKO STOP TAKE CARE. The house where Mitsuko had lived was soon torn down to make room for some apartments, and by the time construction began, the children were all going to new cram schools, and hardly ever ventured into that part of town again.

THE NAKED EYE

Yoko Tawada

Translated by Susan Bernofsky

A suspenseful tale of abduction, obsession, and lost
identity that spans Vietnam, East Berlin, West Germany,
Paris – and fantasies of Catherine Deneuve.

A young Vietnamese woman travels from Ho Chi Minh City to
speak at an International Youth Conference in East Berlin. On her
arrival she is abruptly kidnapped and taken to a small town in West
Germany. One night she (mistakenly) escapes to Paris. Alone, pen-
niless and in a completely foreign land, she wanders the fringes of
society, meeting various shadowy characters. But at the centre of her
new life is Catherine Deneuve, whose films she loses herself in and
who becomes the object of her obsession.

Dreamy, meditative and filled with the gritty everyday perils of
a person living as an illegal alien, *The Naked Eye* is a novel that is as
surprising as it is delightful – each of its thirteen chapters named after
and framed by one of Deneuve's iconic films.

Also available from Granta Books

www.granta.com

THE LAST CHILDREN OF TOKYO

Yoko Tawada

Translated by Margaret Mitsutani

**WINNER OF THE NATIONAL BOOK AWARD
IN TRANSLATED LITERATURE**

'Both unsettling and enchanting, gentle and sharp-edged. Tawada
writes beautifully about unbearable things' Sara Baume

Yoshiro thinks he might never die. A hundred years old and counting,
he is one of Japan's many 'old-elderly'; men and women who remem-
ber a time before terrible catastrophe prompted Japan to shut itself
off from the rest of the world. But while Yoshiro may live, he knows
his beloved great-grandson – born frail and prone to sickness – might
not survive to adulthood.

As hopes for Japan's youngest generation fade, a secretive organ-
isation embarks on an audacious plan to find a cure – might Yoshiro's
great-grandson be the key to saving the last children of Tokyo?

'A mini-epic of eco-terror, family drama and speculative
fiction . . . A book unlike any other' *Guardian*

'Impressive . . . Poetic, strange and melancholy'
Times Literary Supplement

'One of the most thorough and convincingly conceived worlds
I have read . . . Constantly surprising and exciting' Daisy Johnson

Also available from Granta Books

www.granta.com

SCATTERED ALL OVER THE EARTH

Yoko Tawada

Translated by Margaret Mitsutani

'Delightful' *Irish Times*

'Memorable, magical' *Guardian*

Japan has vanished into the sea, remembered only as 'the land of sushi', and Hiruko thinks she might be the last Japanese person left alive. Then, she hears word of Susanoo: a mysterious man, who may be her last chance to once again hear the sounds of her native tongue. Together with a band of new-found friends – including a linguist, a Greenlander masking his nationality, a trans woman, and an employee of Karl Marx's House in Trier – she sets out in pursuit of what's left of her homeland.

A playful novel of mutable identities in a changing world, *Scattered All Over the Earth* is a synaesthetic love song to language and liminality, from a writer of infinite variety and meticulous craft.

'A zig-zagging odyssey that playfully examines language and its borders . . . Strange and new' *Financial Times*

'Engrossing and thought-provoking . . . [A] fascinating near-future tale of language and culture in flux' *Big Issue*

'Mesmerising' *Monocle*

Also available from Granta Books

www.granta.com

SUGGESTED IN THE STARS

Yoko Tawada

Translated by Margaret Mitsutani

The electric sequel to *Scattered All Over the Earth*

Hiruko, from the now-vanished archipelago 'somewhere between China and Polynesia', and her band of friends have searched in vain for someone who speaks her native language. They finally track down Susanoo, a sushi chef from the same nation, but there's a problem – he has lost the power of speech. As the companions set out to help Susanoo regain his voice, encountering magic radios, personality swaps and climate-change worries, their friendship empowers them against despair and sets them to dreaming of a better world. But if Hiruko is ever to hear her mother tongue again, a sceptical aphasia specialist in Copenhagen is her last hope.

Suggested in the Stars carries on the astonishing, intrepid adventures of the band of friends in *Scattered All Over the Earth*, Yoko Tawada's rollicking, touching, cheerfully dystopian novel, and delivers exploits that are even more poignant and shambolic.

Also available from Granta Books

www.granta.com

MEMOIRS OF A POLAR BEAR

Yoko Tawada

Translated by Susan Bernofsky

'Funny, subtle and strangely moving' *Economist*

'Strange . . . exquisite' *New Yorker*

Three bears. The first, a diligent memoirist whose unlikely success forces her to flee Soviet Russia. The second, her daughter, a skilled dancer in an East Berlin circus. The third, Knut, a baby bear born and raised in Berlin Zoo at the beginning of the 21st century.

'Enchanting . . . deliciously whimsical and playful
. . . It's through the eyes of [Tawada's] polar bears
that we see humanity most clearly' *National*

'Tawada brings her fine-nosed, soft-furred beasts to life' *Economist*

'Philosophical, political and often profound . . . rich
in physical sensation and whimsy' *Irish Times*

'Hums with beautiful strangeness' *New York Times Book Review*

'Funny and outrageous . . . Tawada dazzles' *Spectator*

'Magnificent . . . A heartfelt read' *Manchester Evening News*